This book belongs to:

_____

_____

_____

First published in Great Britain 2009 • This edition published 2010 • Text and illustrations copyright © Catherine Rayner 2009

www.littletigerpress.com

LITTLE TIGER PRESS An imprint of Magi Publications, 1 The Coda Centre, 189 Munster Road, London SW6 6AW

A CIP catalogue record for this book is available from the British Library. All rights reserved • ISBN 978-1-84506-857-8 Printed in China

6 8 10 9 7
2 4 5 3

Catherine Rayner has asserted her right to be identified as the author and illustrator of this work under the Copyright, Designs and Patents Act, 1988

For the little ones – Jacob, Sol, Michael and Abbie ~ CR

Sylvia and Bird

Catherine Rayner

LITTLE TIGER PRESS

London

In a faraway place,
on a high mountain-top,
lived a shimmer-shiny
dragon named Sylvia.

Sylvia loved her leafy home,
but sometimes she felt sad.

She had searched the whole world

but never found any other dragons. Sylvia was lonely.

She gave a big,
　　blustery sigh.
Humfff!

And there, under the leaves,
was a small, surprised bird!

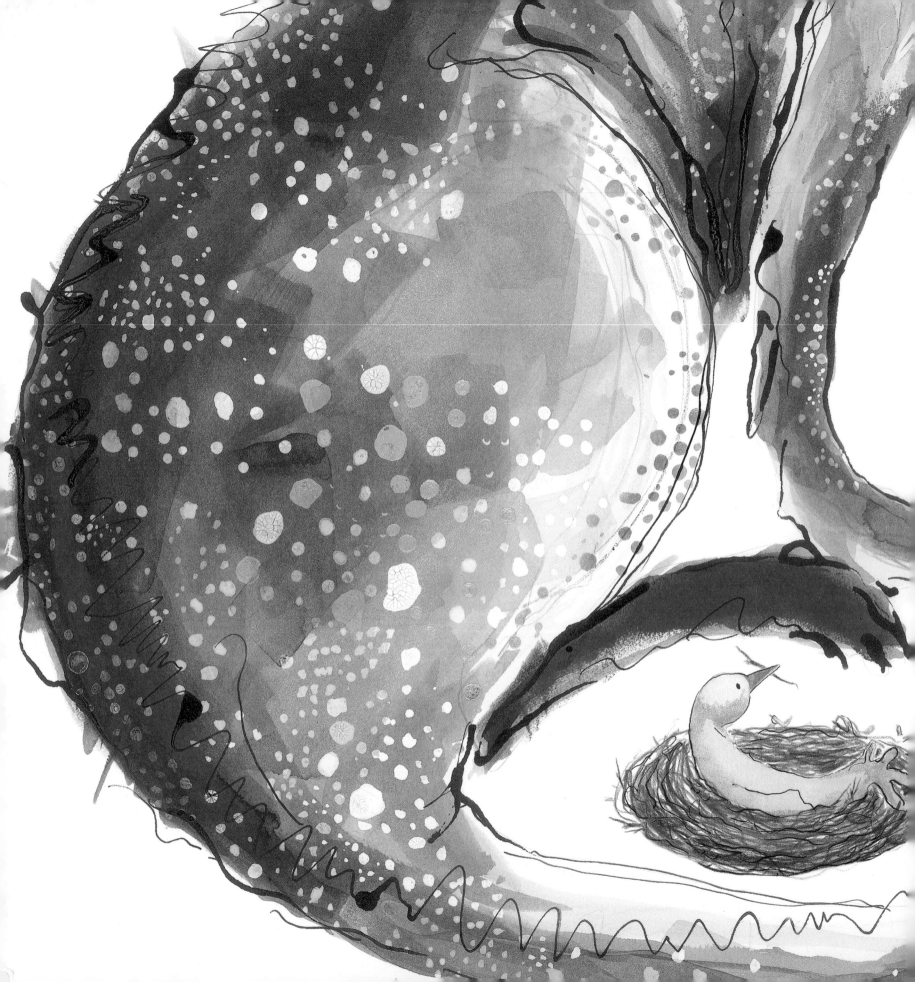

Bird was building a nest, and Sylvia
thought she might be able to help.

Bird and Sylvia became friends.

Being together was so much fun.

Bird and Sylvia spent all their
days together, just like friends do.

But when Bird went to
chit-chatter with the other birds,
Sylvia felt alone.

Bird belonged with the other birds
but Sylvia was different. She had
no dragons to belong with.

Sylvia crept away. She gazed up at the night sky.
Maybe there were other dragons, living on the moon?
She could go and see, but the thought of leaving Bird
made Sylvia feel sadder than ever.

But Bird saw that Sylvia was unhappy.
She had an idea. They would go to the
moon together!

Off they set, racing up through the cool blue skies!

But as Bird and Sylvia
whirled higher and higher
Bird grew cold . . .
        and tired . . .

    Suddenly she
    began to tumble . . .

        down

        down

    down through the clouds . . .

With a cry Sylvia swooped to catch her
tiny friend and gently carried her home.

And there they stayed . . .

. . . for Sylvia realised
she didn't need other dragons
to be happy. The best friend
in the world was loving,
loyal Bird.

Celebrate friendship with
these other books by Little Tiger Press

I Love You as BIG as the World
David Van Buren
Tim Warnes

HARRIS FINDS HIS FEET
CATHERINE RAYNER

Ted, Bo and Diz
The First Adventure
Jason Chapman

THE LAMB WHO CAME FOR DINNER

For information regarding any of the above titles
or for our catalogue, please contact us:
Little Tiger Press, 1 The Coda Centre, 189 Munster Road, London SW6 6AW
Tel: 020 7385 6333 Fax: 020 7385 7333
E-mail: info@littletiger.co.uk • www.littletigerpress.com